THE TALE
OF
PETER RABBIT

THE TALE OF
PETER RABBIT

BY

BEATRIX POTTER

FREDERICK WARNE

The reproductions in this book have been made using
the most modern electronic scanning methods from entirely
new transparencies of Beatrix Potter's original watercolours.
They enable Beatrix Potter's skill as an artist to be appreciated
as never before, not even during her own lifetime.

FREDERICK WARNE

Published by the Penguin Group
27 Wrights Lane, London W8 5TZ, England
Penguin Books USA Inc., 375 Hudson Street, New York, New York 10014, USA
Penguin Books Australia Ltd, Ringwood, Victoria, Australia
Penguin Books Canada Ltd, 10 Alcorn Avenue, Toronto, Ontario, Canada M4V 3B2
Penguin Books (NZ) Ltd, 182-190 Wairau Road, Auckland 10, New Zealand

Penguin Books Ltd, Registered Offices: Harmondsworth, Middlesex, England

First published 1902
Published with new reproductions 1987
This edition first published in paperback 1991
This hardcover edition first published 1992

Printed and bound in Great Britain by
William Clowes Limited, Beccles and London

0592

8

ONCE upon a time there were four little Rabbits, and their names were—

> Flopsy,
> Mopsy,
> Cotton-tail,
> and Peter.

They lived with their Mother in a sand-bank, underneath the root of a very big fir-tree.

'NOW, my dears,' said old Mrs. Rabbit one morning, ' you may go into the fields or down the lane, but don't go into Mr. McGregor's garden: your Father had an accident there; he was put in a pie by Mrs. McGregor.'

11

12

' NOW run along, and don't get into mischief. I am going out.'

THEN old Mrs. Rabbit took a basket and her umbrella, and went through the wood to the baker's. She bought a loaf of brown bread and five currant buns.

15

16

FLOPSY, Mopsy, and Cotton-
tail, who were good little
bunnies, went down the lane to
gather blackberries:

BUT Peter, who was very naughty, ran straight away to Mr. McGregor's garden, and squeezed under the gate!

19

20

FIRST he ate some lettuces
and some French beans;
and then he ate some radishes;

AND then, feeling rather sick, he went to look for some parsley.

22

23

24

BUT round the end of a cucumber frame, whom should he meet but Mr. McGregor!

MR. McGREGOR was on his hands and knees planting out young cabbages, but he jumped up and ran after Peter, waving a rake and calling out, ' Stop thief! '

28

PETER was most dreadfully frightened; he rushed all over the garden, for he had forgotten the way back to the gate.

He lost one of his shoes among the cabbages, and the other shoe amongst the potatoes.

AFTER losing them, he ran on four legs and went faster, so that I think he might have got away altogether if he had not unfortunately run into a gooseberry net, and got caught by the large buttons on his jacket. It was a blue jacket with brass buttons, quite new.

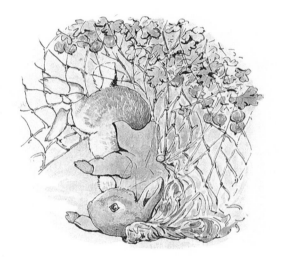

31

32

PETER gave himself up for lost, and shed big tears; but his sobs were overheard by some friendly sparrows, who flew to him in great excitement, and implored him to exert himself.

MR. McGREGOR came up
with a sieve, which he
intended to pop upon the top
of Peter; but Peter wriggled
out just in time, leaving his
jacket behind him.

34

35

A ND rushed into the tool-
shed, and jumped into a
can. It would have been a
beautiful thing to hide in, if it
had not had so much water in
it.

MR. McGREGOR was quite sure that Peter was somewhere in the tool-shed, perhaps hidden underneath a flower-pot. He began to turn them over carefully, looking under each.

Presently Peter sneezed— ' Kertyschoo! ' Mr. McGregor was after him in no time.

39

40

AND tried to put his foot upon Peter, who jumped out of a window, upsetting three plants. The window was too small for Mr. McGregor, and he was tired of running after Peter. He went back to his work.

PETER sat down to rest;
he was out of breath and
trembling with fright, and he
had not the least idea which
way to go. Also he was very
damp with sitting in that can.

After a time he began to
wander about, going lippity—
lippity—not very fast, and looking all round.

44

HE found a door in a wall; but it was locked, and there was no room for a fat little rabbit to squeeze underneath.

An old mouse was running in and out over the stone doorstep, carrying peas and beans to her family in the wood. Peter asked her the way to the gate, but she had such a large pea in her mouth that she could not answer. She only shook her head at him. Peter began to cry.

THEN he tried to find his way straight across the garden, but he became more and more puzzled. Presently, he came to a pond where Mr. McGregor filled his water-cans. A white cat was staring at some gold-fish, she sat very, very still, but now and then the tip of her tail twitched as if it were alive. Peter thought it best to go away without speaking to her; he had heard about cats from his cousin, little Benjamin Bunny.

48

HE went back towards the tool-shed, but suddenly, quite close to him, he heard the noise of a hoe—scr-r-ritch, scratch, scratch, scritch. Peter scuttered underneath the bushes. But presently, as nothing happened, he came out, and climbed upon a wheel-barrow and peeped over. The first thing he saw was Mr. McGregor hoeing onions. His back was turned towards Peter, and beyond him was the gate!

49

PETER got down very
quietly off the wheelbarrow,
and started running as fast as
he could go, along a straight
walk behind some black-currant
bushes.

Mr. McGregor caught sight
of him at the corner, but Peter
did not care. He slipped underneath the gate, and was safe at
last in the wood outside the
garden.

51

M R. McGREGOR hung up
the little jacket and the
shoes for a scare-crow to
frighten the blackbirds.

PETER never stopped run-
ning or looked behind him
till he got home to the big
fir-tree.

He was so tired that he
flopped down upon the nice
soft sand on the floor of the
rabbit-hole and shut his eyes.
His mother was busy cooking;
she wondered what he had done
with his clothes. It was the
second little jacket and pair of
shoes that Peter had lost in a
fortnight!

55

I AM sorry to say that Peter was not very well during the evening.

His mother put him to bed, and made some camomile tea; and she gave a dose of it to Peter!

'One table-spoonful to be taken at bed-time.'

58

BUT Flopsy, Mopsy, and Cotton-tail had bread and milk and blackberries for supper.

THE END